Dick Bruna

Miffy
Goes Flying

Dick Bruna Books, Inc.
PRICE/STERN/SLOAN
Publishers, Inc., Los Angeles
1984

Miffy was playing on the grass.

Her long ears heard a sound.

A very funny noise

seemed to come from all around.

A plane was flying through the air.

Miffy looked up at the sky.

Her uncle was the pilot.

He was flying very high.

The plane came in for a landing.

When it was safely down,

Miffy called, "Hi, Uncle!

What brings you to town?"

"Well," he said to Miffy.

"Would you like to come with me

and fly high through the air

over mountains and the sea?"

"Whoopee!" shouted Miffy.

"That will be great fun,

but maybe first I'd better

go and ask my mom."

She quickly ran to ask her mother.

She said yes, provided that

Miffy would first run and get

her warmest woolen hat.

Moments later, up they went

in her uncle's flying machine.

"Isn't it wonderful," Miffy thought,

"I hope it's not a dream!"

"We are up so high, Uncle,"

said Miffy, feeling very brave.

Far below she saw

her tiny mother wave.

"Look at all those trees," said her uncle.

"If you look closely, you could

see a beautiful castle

in the middle of the wood."

"Look at the sea!" cried Miffy.

She pointed to a place

where five small sailboats

were having a race.

"I think we had better go home,"

Uncle said to Miffy.

"That is too bad," she replied.

"Time passed in such a jiffy."

Miffy told her mother,

"It seemed like a dream.

I like having an uncle

with his own flying machine!"

Books by Dick Bruna:

The Apple
The Little Bird
Lisa and Lynn
The Fish
Miffy
Miffy at the Zoo
Miffy in the Snow
Miffy at the Seaside
I Can Read
I Can Read More
A Story to Tell
I Can Count
Snuffy
Snuffy and the Fire
Miffy Goes Flying

Miffy's Birthday
I Can Count More
Animal Book
Miffy at the Playground
Miffy in the Hospital
Miffy's Dream
When I'm Big
I Know about Numbers
I Know More about Numbers
I Know about Shapes
Farmer John
Miffy's Bicycle
The Rescue
The Orchestra
Miffy Goes to School

First published in the U.S.A. 1984
by Dick Bruna Books Inc., New York
Illustrations Dick Bruna
Copyright Mercis bv., Amsterdam © 1970, all rights reserved
Text copyright © Dick Bruna 1984
Exclusively arranged and produced by Mercis Publishing bv., Amsterdam
Printed and bound by Brepols Fabrieken nv., Turnhout, Belgium
I.S.B.N. 0-8431-1535-1